This book belongs to:

....

....

For Alison Sage M.W.

First published in 2013 by Hodder Children's Books
This paperback edition published in 2014

Text copyright © Martin Waddell 2013
Illustrations copyright © Lee Wildish 2013

Hodder Children's Books, 338 Euston Road, London, NW1 3BH
Hodder Children's Books Australia, Level 17/207 Kent Street,
Sydney, NSW 2000

ISBN 978 1 444 90679 0

Printed in China

Hodder Children's Books is a division of Hachette Children's Books,
an Hachette UK Company

www.hachette.co.uk

Bears, Bears, Bears!

Martin Waddell and Lee Wildish

A division of Hachette Children's Books

Ruby liked bears so she put up a sign.

Along came a bear.
"I'm a bear from Bear Wood,"
said the bear. "Will I do?"

"You're just what I wanted," said Ruby.
Ruby and the bear played games:

bear hug...

bear chase...

and bear hide-and-seek.

"More bears!"
cried Ruby.

"Am I not enough?"
asked Ruby's bear.

94, 95, 96, 97

"More bears mean more fun!" cried Ruby. So Ruby's bear sent out to Bear Wood for more bears.

Two little bears came from Bear Wood and they played with Ruby.

"More! More!" cried Ruby. So Ruby's bear sent out to Bear Wood again and a bunch of party-loving, ring-a-ding bears turned up.

One cool bear played the piano and sang, and some of them danced on the patio.

They all wanted to dance with Ruby, and they whirled and twirled until she was puffed.

But she still cried,

"More! More! More!"

And more and more bears came from Bear Wood.

Some of them took
Ruby paddling down
at the creek.

The moon rose over Bear Wood
as Ruby came sleepily home.

Back at her house, the bear party was still going on. There were bears in the cupboards and bears on the stairs. Bears looking at pictures and climbing on chairs. There were bears everywhere!

Five bears were snoring in Ruby's bed.
"I'll sleep in the bath!"
Ruby said, grabbing a
blanket off the bears.

But there was a bear in the bath playing with boats. Two bears were queuing to get in the shower. Three bears were looking for towels. And the littlest of all the bears was curled up in the basin.

"THERE ARE TOO MANY BEARS!"

cried Ruby.

"I thought there might be,"
said Ruby's bear. And he yelled:
"BEARS OUT!"

Straight away the
bears hurtled out
of Ruby's house.

Bears **climbed** through the windows.

Bears **squeezed** up the chimney.

Bears **shot** through the doors.

Bears **popped** out from under the floors.

Everywhere there were bears,
running off into Bear Wood!

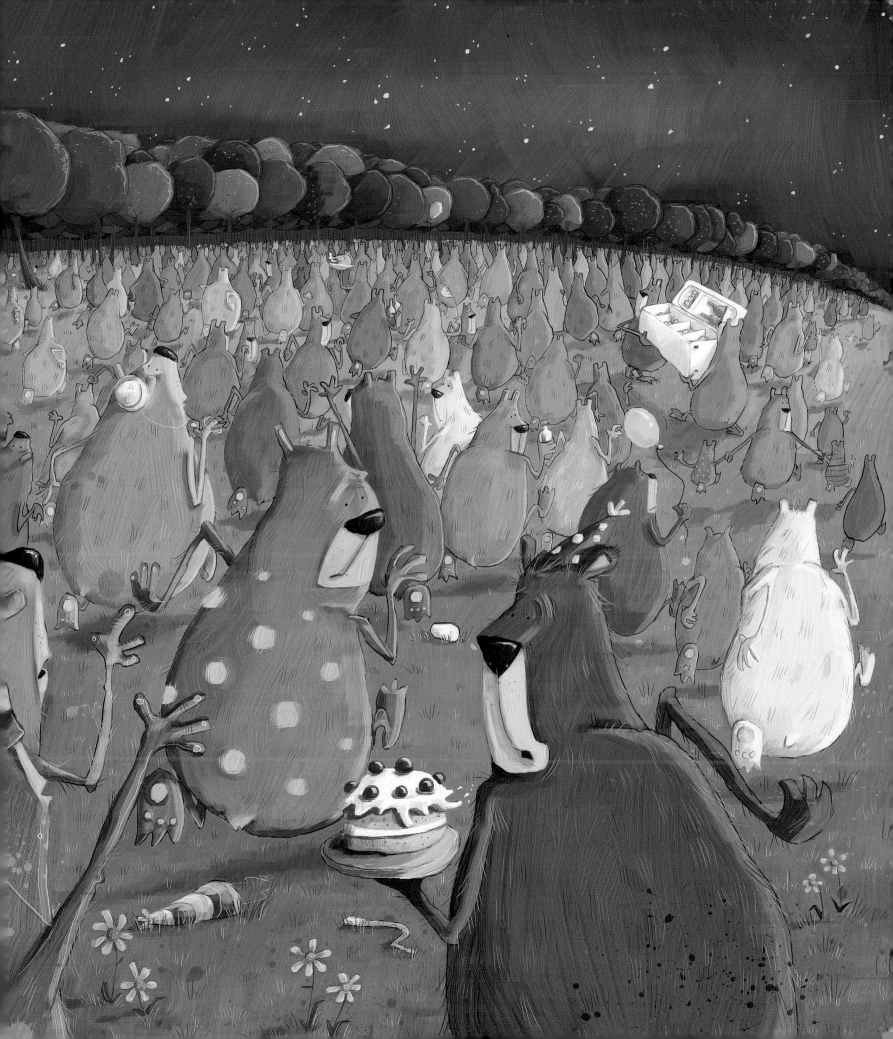

"Now you've only one bear left," said Ruby's bear.

"One bear is just what I wanted," said Ruby.

If you enjoyed this wonderful book,
you'll love . . .

978 0 340 95711 0

Kes Gray
MUM
AND
DAD
GLUE
Illustrated by
Lee Wildish

978 0 340 98128 3

Friendly Day
MIJ KELLY   CHARLES FUGE

978 1 444 90015 6

Kes Gray and Lee Wildish
Leave Me
Alone
A tale of what happens when you face up to a bully

978 1 444 90158 0

COPYCAT BEAR!
Ellie Sandall

978 1 444 91588 4

Illustrated by
the winner of the
Red House
Children's Book
Award
HOW TO
BABYSIT
A
GRANDAD
by JEAN REAGAN   illustrated by LEE WILDISH

978 0 340 98839 8

Jacob
O'Reilly
Wants
a Pet
Lynne
Rickards
and Lee
Wildish